No Help Wanted!

Ruth Ohi

Scholastic Canada Ltd.
Toronto New York London Auckland Sydney
Mexico City New Delhi Hong Kong Buenos Aires

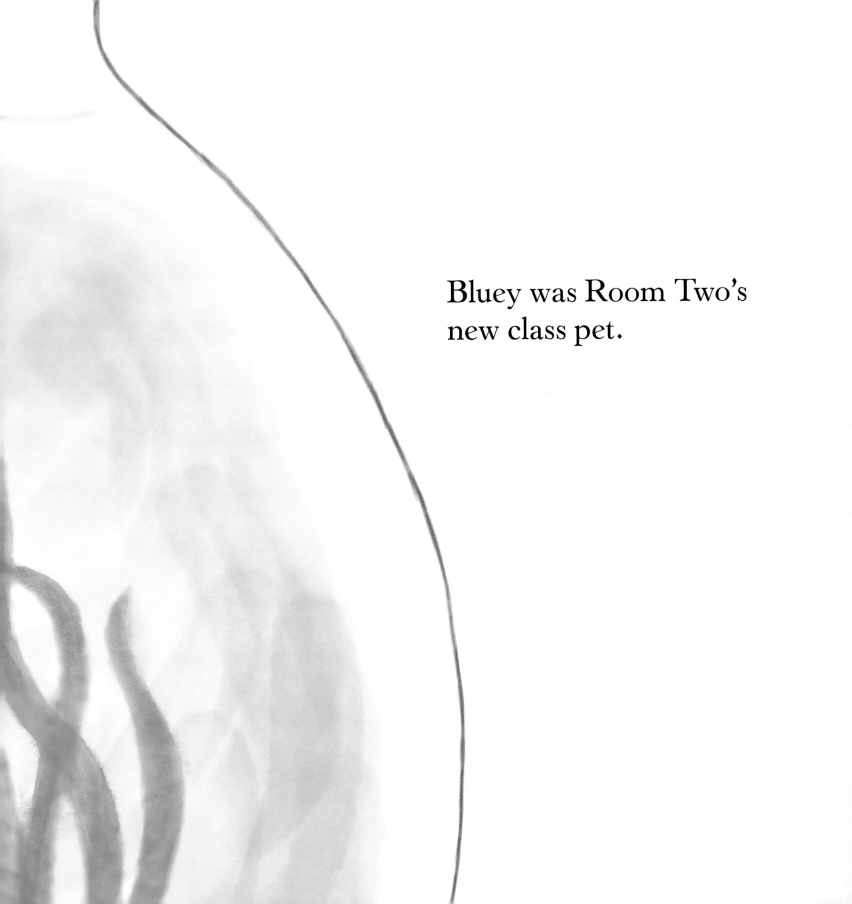

Bluey was Room Two's
new class pet.

Mr. Zen talked about how someone needed to feed Bluey every day.

Posy was very keen.

Posy picked the fanciest food flakes for Bluey.

Posy provided stimulation
so Bluey was never bored.

"We can all be friends!" growled Posy
in her best Monster Shark voice.

The following day, Jacob said, "I made a puppet too."

"I'll take that!" said Posy. "This will help with the parade scene."

"I think Bluey needs a checkup," said
Sam. "I'm a vet. May I take a look?"

"I'll do it," said Posy.
"You'll scare her."

"All you need is me," said Posy.

But Bluey was not looking
that well.

Posy formed
each food flake
into a tiny tiara.

But Bluey was not impressed.

The next day, Posy staged a
full-scale, fish-themed musical.

But still Bluey looked unwell.

"Everyone will blame me!" thought Posy.

So Posy hid Bluey.

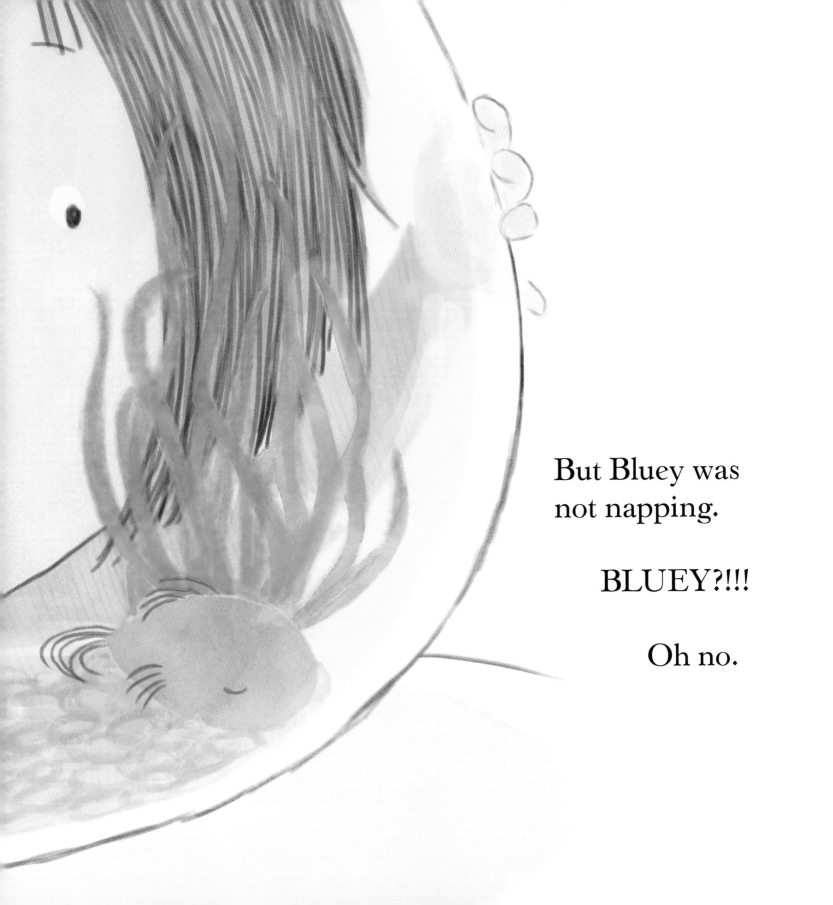

But Bluey was
not napping.

BLUEY?!!!

Oh no.

Posy knew what she had to do.

The class came
and helped.

Bluey started looking better.

So did Posy.

"You are a great fish friend," said Mr. Zen. "Thanks for letting us help."

The following week was Jacob's turn.
Posy had lots of helpful tips.

And the class couldn't help noticing
that Bluey always seemed to enjoy. . .

. . . a good puppet show.

For Hewitt, Alexandra, Maeve,
Charlie and Ian

Scholastic Canada Ltd.
604 King Street West, Toronto, Ontario M5V 1E1, Canada

Scholastic Inc.
557 Broadway, New York, NY 10012, USA

Scholastic Australia Pty Limited
PO Box 579, Gosford, NSW 2250, Australia

Scholastic New Zealand Limited
Private Bag 94407, Botany, Manukau 2163, New Zealand

Scholastic Children's Books
Euston House, 24 Eversholt Street, London NW1 1DB, UK

www.scholastic.ca

Library and Archives Canada Cataloguing in Publication

Ohi, Ruth, author, illustrator
No help wanted! / [written and illustrated by] Ruth Ohi.

Published simultaneously in hardcover by North Winds Press.
ISBN 978-1-4431-6361-3 (softcover)

I. Title.

PS8579.H47N6 2019b   jC813'.6   C2018-906335-1

Author photo by Annie T.

6 5 4 3 2 1   Printed in Malaysia 108   19 20 21 22 23